PATRIOTIC SYMBOLS

The National Anthem

Nancy Harris

Heinemann Library
Chicago, Illinois

HEINEMANN-RAINTREE

TO ORDER:
☎ Phone Customer Service **888-454-2279**
💻 Visit **www.heinemannraintree.com** to browse our catalog and order online.

Editorial: Rebecca Rissman
Design: Kimberly R. Miracle
Photo Research: Tracy Cummins and Heather Mauldin
Production: Duncan Gilbert

Originated by Dot Gradations
Printed and bound in China by South China Printing Co. Ltd.
The paper used to print this book comes from sustainable resources.

ISBN-13: 978-1-4329-0965-9 (hc)
ISBN-10: 1-4329-0965-7 (hc)
ISBN-13: 978-1-4329-0972-7 (pb)
ISBN-10: 1-4329-0972-X (pb)

12 11 10 09 08
10 9 8 7 6 5 4 3 2 1

Cataloging-in-Publication data avaiable at Library of Congress:loc.gov

Acknowledgments
The author and publisher are grateful to the following for permission to reproduce copyright material: ©Age Fotostock **p. 4** (Maurizio Borsari); ©AP Photo **p. 9** (The News & Observer/Chuck Liddy); ©Corbis **pp. 16** (Bettmann), **17** (Smithsonian Institution); ©Getty Images **pp. 8** (AFP/Henry Ray Abrams), **13** (Stephen Lovekin), **18** (Shaun Botterill), **19** (David Stuka), **21, 23b** (Chung Sung-Jun); ©The Granger Collection, New York **pp. 6, 10, 14, 20**; ©Shutterstock **pp. 5** top right (Aravind Balaraman), **5** bottom right (Raymond Kasprzak), **5** bottom left (ExaMedia Photography), **5** top left (Stephen Finn), 7 (Jamie Cross), **11**.

Cover image used with permission of ©AP Photo (Chris Gardner). Back cover image used with permission of ©Age Fotostock (Maurizio Borsari).

The publishers would like to thank Nancy Harris for her assistance in the preparation of this book.

Every effort has been made to contact copyright holders of any material reproduced in this book. Any omissions will be rectified in subsequent printings if notice is given to the publisher.

Disclaimer
All the Internet addresses (URLs) given in this book were valid at the time of going to press. However, due to the dynamic nature of the Internet, some addresses may have changed, or sites may have changed or ceased to exist since publication. While the author and publisher regret any inconvenience this may cause readers, no responsibility for any such changes can be accepted by either the author or the publisher.

Contents

What Is a Symbol?

The National Anthem is a symbol.
A symbol is a type of sign.

A symbol shows you something.
A symbol can have words.

The National Anthem

The National Anthem is a song.

It is a special symbol.

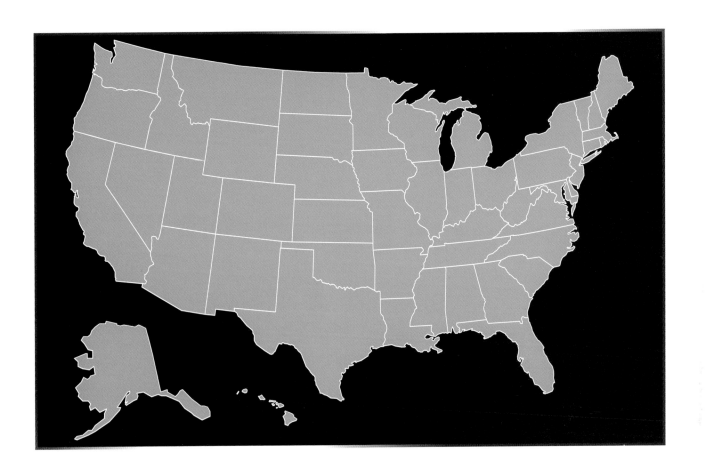

It is a symbol of the United States of America.
The United States of America is a country.

The National Anthem is a patriotic symbol.

The song shows the beliefs of the country.
The United States is a free country.

Star Spangled Banner

O say can you see ~~through~~ by the dawn's early light,
What so proudly we hail'd at the twilight's last gleaming,
Whose broad stripes & bright stars through the perilous fight
O'er the ramparts we watch'd, were so gallantly streaming?
And the rocket's red glare, the bomb bursting in air,
Gave proof through the night that our flag was still there,
O say does that star spangled banner yet wave
O'er the land of the free & the home of the brave?

On the shore dimly seen through the mists of the deep,
Where the foe's haughty host in dread silence reposes,
What is that which the breeze, o'er the towering steep,
As it fitfully blows, half conceals, half discloses?
Now it catches the gleam

The name of the song is the Star Spangled Banner.

The star spangled banner is the American Flag.

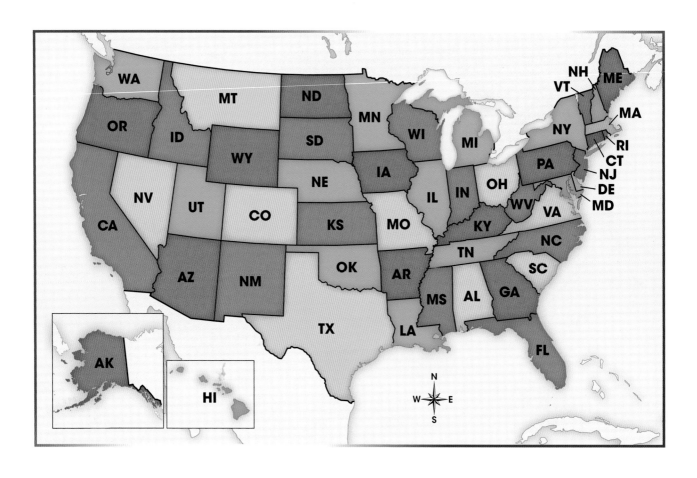

The song is about the United States of America.

The song is about freedom.

Battle of 1812

"And the rocket's red glare, the bombs bursting in air…"

The words tell how the United States fought to stay free.

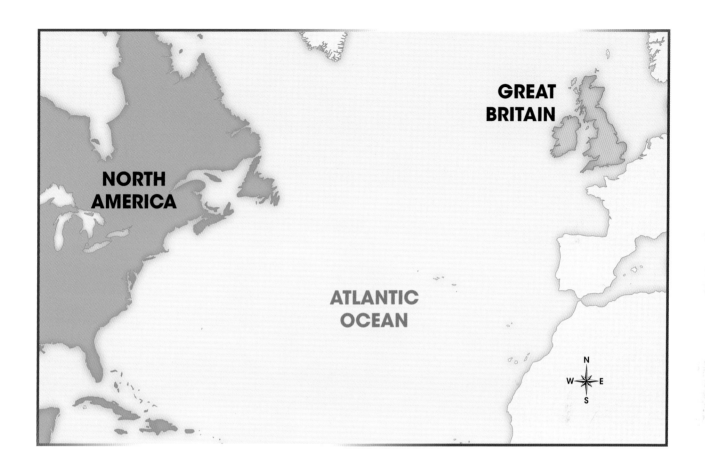

The United States fought Great Britain.

"...our flag was still there."

The words tell how the flag was still flying after a big battle.

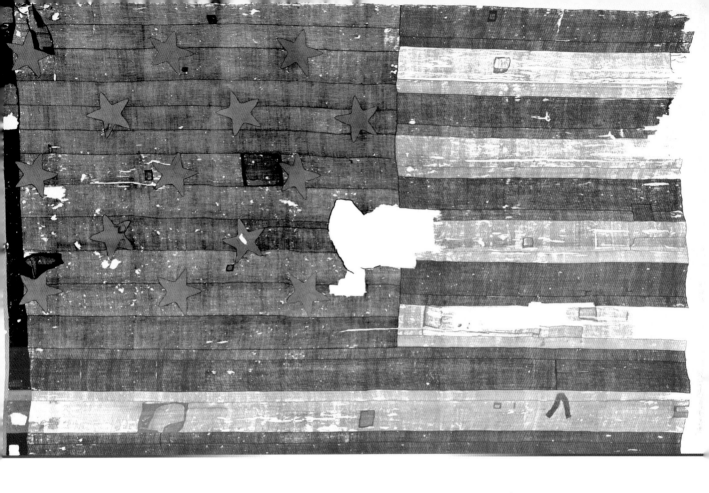

The flag is a symbol of the country's freedom.

The National Anthem Today

People stand when the National Anthem is played.

They stand and look at the American flag.

What It Tells You

"The land of the free..."

The song tells you how the United States fought to stay a free country.

" ...and the home of the brave! "

The song shows you how important freedom is to people in the United States.

National Anthem Facts

★ The National Anthem was written by Francis Scott Key. He wrote the words in 1814.

★ It became the National Anthem in 1931.

★ The American Flag in the song is on display in the National Museum of History. This museum is in Washington, D.C., the nation's capital.

Glossary

country
area of land governed by the same leader or group

patriotic
believing in your country

Index

Note to Parents and Teachers

The study of patriotic symbols introduces young readers to our country's government and history. Books in this series begin by defining a symbol before focusing on the history and significance of a specific patriotic symbol. Use the facts section on page 22 to introduce readers to these non-fiction features.

The text has been carefully chosen with the advice of a literacy expert to enable beginning readers success while reading independently or with moderate support. An expert in the field of early childhood social studies curriculum was consulted to provide interesting and appropriate content.

You can support children's nonfiction literacy skills by helping students use the table of contents, headings, picture glossary, and index.